Lesson from Lester

Jan Burchett and Sara Vogler
Illustrated by Teri Gower

Lester was a big cat. He had a warm home. He had good dinners and he had a kind family. His family gave him everything he wanted.

3

There were three people in Lester's family. There was one called Mum and one called Dad. There was also one called Milly. Milly was very clever. She was almost as clever as a cat.

Lester had taught his family well. They could sharpen their claws — just like he did. They could sleep on pillows — just like he did. They could play with toys — just like he did.

Lester should have been a happy cat. He had everything a cat could want. But Lester was not happy. There was one thing his family couldn't do — one very big thing. They couldn't catch mice!

Lester decided he would have to teach his family to catch mice. They would like that.

Lester tried to teach Mum to catch mice. He showed her how to keep quiet. He showed her how to hide.

When a mouse came out of its hole, Lester showed Mum how to catch it. But Mum was no good at it.

"Oh, no!" cried Lester in a loud meow. "That's no good. You're blocking the hole!"

Next, Lester tried to teach Dad to catch mice. He showed him how to keep quiet. He showed him how to hide.

When a mouse came out from under the oven, Lester showed Dad how to pounce. But Dad was no good at it.

"No, no, no!" cried Lester in a loud meow. "You can't pounce from up there!"

Lester was not happy. Mum and Dad could not catch mice. But there was still Milly. She was almost as clever as a cat! Lester decided to teach Milly to catch mice.

Lester showed Milly how to keep quiet. He showed her how to hide. Next, he showed her how to pounce.

When a mouse came out from under the shed, Lester showed Milly how to catch it. But even Milly was no good at it.

"Keep quiet!" said Lester in a very loud meow. "You'll scare the mouse!"

Lester was not happy. No one in his family could catch mice. Lester's family was kind. They tried to make him happy. They gave him a good dinner but Lester wouldn't eat it.

16

17

Then they gave him a new scratching post, but Lester wouldn't scratch it.

Next, they gave him a new pillow, but Lester wouldn't sleep on it.

Lester was still not happy. He was sleeping when he heard a strange ringing. He looked up. Milly had something strange in her paws. She showed it to him. Lester looked at it with one eye.

It was a strange mouse. It didn't smell like a mouse and it had a bell on its tail. But it was big and fat and it was a mouse! Milly could catch mice!

Lester was very happy with Milly. He had always known she was the clever one.

Lester was very happy. At last, someone in his family could catch mice!